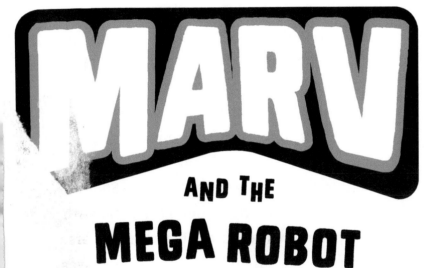

MARV

AND THE

MEGA ROBOT

DEAR READER,

I've always wanted to be a superhero. I think that's what drew me to writing Marv. You can find countless pictures of me as a child dressed up in superhero costumes. I think that's pretty common right now, but what you have to understand is that when I grew up, I didn't have Marvel superhero movies coming out every other month—I had to make do with comics and cartoons.

One of those cartoons was called *Static Shock*. Its superhero was Static, a young black kid with electric powers who spouted cheesy one-liners as he zapped bad guys. Watching that show was the first time I had ever seen a young black boy be the hero of anything I'd ever watched or read. There was a reverence in the way that me and my friends watched and talked about *Static Shock*. We didn't have the language at that age to talk about representation and its importance, but deep down I know we all felt the same thing.

Static is a superhero, and he looks like us and that's really cool. He's one of us.

Quite a few years have passed since I was a kid watching *Static Shock*, and unfortunately, we don't have that many more prominent black superheroes. I cannot click my fingers and change this—after all, I am *not* a superhero. However, I feel that, by writing Marv and detailing his adventures, the laughs, and the struggles, I might give kids today the feeling I had all those years ago when I watched *Static Shock.*

Marv is a superhero, and he looks like us and that's really cool. He's one of us.

I hope you enjoy the book as much as I enjoyed writing it.

Alex

That's me!

OXFORD
UNIVERSITY PRESS

Great Clarendon Street, Oxford OX2 6DP
Oxford University Press is a department of the University of Oxford.
It furthers the University's objective of excellence in research, scholarship,
and education by publishing worldwide. Oxford is a registered trade mark
of Oxford University Press in the UK and in certain other countries

Database right Oxford University Press (maker)

First published in 2022

British Library Cataloguing in Publication Data

Data available

ISBN: 978-0-19-278042-3

3 5 7 9 10 8 6 4 2

Printed and bound by CPI Group (UK) Ltd, Croydon, CR0 4YY

Paper used in the production of this book is a natural,
recyclable product made from wood grown in sustainable forests.
The manufacturing process conforms to the environmental
regulations of the country of origin.

MARV

AND THE
MEGA ROBOT

WRITTEN BY
ALEX FALASE-KOYA

PICTURES BY
PAULA BOWLES

OXFORD
UNIVERSITY PRESS

CHAPTER 1

Marvin carefully fixed the head onto the small robot. If they could make the robot work this time, Marv and his best friend Joe would be entering it into the school Science Fair tomorrow. The thought made Marvin feel excited and nervous all at the same time. The small robot was made of old bits of scrap metal, and Joe and Marvin had been working hard on it for weeks now.

The two friends glanced at each other and nodded. It was time to test it out. Marvin took a deep breath and leant forward, pressing a button on the back of the robot. Its small square head sprang up.

'Readaloud 3000 powering on,'

the robot said in a stiff voice.
Marvin grinned at Joe. It was working!

A blue beam came from the robot's round glass eyes. Marvin slid a piece of paper across the desk for the robot to read.

'Baa, baa, black sheep, have you any wool?'

the robot said slowly, reading the words on the paper. Marvin and Joe grabbed each other and leapt up and down.

'Yes! We did it!' they shouted, too excited to notice the curious looks from their classmates.

'Yes, sir, Yes, sir, three bags full.'

The robot's voice began to rise higher and higher with each word that passed.

Marvin and Joe stopped jumping.

'Is it supposed to do that?' Marvin said.

'I don't think so.' Joe tapped the robot, and it began to vibrate.

The robot shuddered as it rocketed through the words:

'Oneforthemasterandonefor thedameandoneforthelittleboy.

'Something's wrong!' Joe said,
stumbling back. 'Do something, Marvin!'

'We need to turn it off!' Marvin said, leaping forward, but before he could touch it, a puff of smoke came out of the little robot and its head sunk down.

The teacher, Ms Davis, came over to their table. 'Sorry boys, it looks as though your robot has had another short circuit.'

'It broke again,' Joe whispered. The whole classroom had stopped working on their inventions and were staring at Joe and Marvin. 'What if we can't fix it in time for the Science Fair tomorrow?'

'It's alright Joe. I think we just need to work on it a little bit more.' Marvin nodded confidently, but inside he wasn't sure there was anything more they could do.

'That piece of rust is never going to

work!' another boy in their class called over. A few of his friends began to giggle.

Marvin put his hand on Joe's shoulder.

'Don't worry about him.' Marvin smiled. 'We'll get there eventually. We just need to try again.'

'I guess you're right,' Joe replied.

Marvin and Joe worked on repairing their invention until it was lunchtime and then headed to the school hall.

Joe laid out a mountain of superhero comics in front of them as they opened their lunchboxes.

'There are so many of them,' Marvin exclaimed.

'I told you I had a lot.' Joe nudged him. 'My nan remembers when there were real superheroes living in the city. These are all their stories.'

Marvin and Joe flicked through the comics. Joe occasionally blurted out a 'so cool' when something caught his eye. Marvin was quiet though—nothing really stood out to him. Until ... he saw it.

'Who's that?' Marvin picked up a
tattered comic from the pile. There was
a tall superhero on the cover, wearing a
blue suit with a large 'M' on the front. He
had dark skin just like Marvin and he
looked familiar somehow.

'That's one of my oldest comics. His name is—'

'Marv,' Marvin said, reading the title of the comic aloud.

'What if we got to be superheroes one day?' Joe grabbed Marvin's arm excitedly, with a wide grin on his face. 'What powers would you have if you were a superhero?' Joe didn't wait for Marvin to respond. 'What about flying? Or super climbing? Or super speed? Or even invisibility!'

'A mixture of all those things would be cool,' Marvin said with a grin.

'How about the power to make our robot the most awesome invention of them all at the Science Fair? We would crush the competition!'

Marvin laughed. Joe really wanted to win.

It wasn't the first time Marvin had thought about what superpowers he'd want. Secretly, he loved the idea of being a superhero. But he wasn't big, or strong, or even that brave. Did he actually have what it takes? Marvin wasn't so sure.

In the afternoon, Marvin and Joe put the finishing touches to their robot. They would just have to hope that it worked at the Science Fair.

At home time, Marvin's grandad was waiting for him at the school gates.

'Where's Dad?' Marvin asked.

'He had another late shift at the hospital today, so you're stuck with me again.' Marvin felt the edges of his mouth curl downwards. It had been a couple of days since he last got to hang out with his dad.

'Hey—I bet it feels good to know your dad is a hero. That's what nurses are, you know. But I can see you feel a bit sad that he's at work again. Come and give your grandad a big hug!' Grandad always knew how Marvin was feeling, even when Marvin didn't know himself. It was like Grandad's superpower.

'I won't frown,' Marvin said, a smile beginning to form on his face as they set off for home together.

'Promise?' Grandad said.

'Promise,' Marvin said.

At home, Grandad put some music on while he made dinner. He left his thick sunglasses on even though they were inside.

'Hey Grandad,' Marv said.

'Hey little one,' Grandad replied.

'You know it's the Science Fair tomorrow? Me and Joe are entering our robot, but it broke again today. It might have exploded, but only a little bit … It's not really dangerous or anything, I promise,' Marvin added quickly.

'Nothing wrong with a little bit of danger every now and again.' Grandad pulled down his sunglasses and winked.

Marvin giggled, then stopped. A memory from earlier was in his head.

'A kid in our class was mean about our invention. I told Joe not to worry about it, but maybe I should have done more. Maybe I should have—'

Grandad raised a hand, interrupting Marvin.

'Come over here,' Grandad said. Marvin got up and walked towards him. Grandad wrapped Marvin up in a warm hug. 'The heroic thing isn't to start a fight, it's to be a good friend, and that's what you did.' Grandad let go, then reached out and patted Marvin's

chest. 'Your big heart, little one. That's your superpower.'

'Can that really be a superpower?' Marvin said with a smile, staring up at Grandad.

'Of course, it can. And I think you'd make a great superhero one day.' Grandad pulled down his sunglasses and gave another wink.

'But superheroes don't even exist any more.'

'That is true.' Grandad looked at Marvin and grinned. 'But maybe it's time for that to change ... Could you do me a favour, Marvin? Go into the loft and bring down my old brown suitcase. I have some keepsakes in there I want to share with you.'

Feeling puzzled, Marvin went upstairs, then up the thin ladder into the loft. It was dark and filled with cobwebs and dusty boxes. He had no idea how many spiders or other creepy-crawlies were up here. Part of him wanted to leave, but Grandad only asked him to get the suitcase. He couldn't turn back without even trying.

Marvin took a couple of steps, then his foot hit something, and he almost fell.

Grandad's brown suitcase lay at Marvin's feet, covered in a thick layer of dust. Marvin tried to lift it, but it was surprisingly heavy. He shook it, and it rattled. What was inside? There was only one way to find out.

Marvin reached down and opened the suitcase. Inside was a piece of clothing. Marvin held it up ... It was a dull blue colour with a huge 'M' on the front. His jaw dropped. It looked a bit like a superhero outfit!

CHAPTER 2

The super-suit looked way too big for Marvin, but he couldn't resist. He had to try it on!

Marvin slipped the suit on over his clothes. The long fabric of the legs and arms flopped over his hands and feet. Marvin laughed; he was practically drowning in the suit. Just as he was about to take it off, the super-suit suddenly changed. Its arms and legs shrunk until they were exactly Marvin's size. He stared at the suit in amazement. It fit him perfectly now.

With all that extra fabric out of the way, Marvin could see a button on the suit's chest. Marvin didn't stop to think. He just pressed it.

A whirring sound came from the suit. It sounded as though it was waking up. It shifted and crackled, tickling Marvin.

The suit was no longer a dull colour. It was bright blue with a huge, flashing 'M' on the front. Marvin had seen this somewhere before. It looked exactly like Marv's suit from the comic book!

Suddenly, there was a noise from the suitcase. Marvin looked down and noticed there was something else in the case. A small, round robot. And it

seemed to be whirring to life.

'Wha—?' Marvin exclaimed, jumping back.

'Apologies,' a robotic voice replied. 'I lose control of my beeping module when my excitement levels are over 9000.' The robot beeped again loudly, five more times.

'Woah.' Marvin took a deep breath and crouched down to get a closer look at the robot.

It had both a round body and a small round head. It

was silvery and smooth with long ridged arms and huge round eyes. The robot sat up and then hovered effortlessly off the ground, so it was level with Marvin's face. It was so high-tech. How did something so cool end up in the loft?!

'New superhero detected!' the robot said loudly, and then beeped a couple more times. 'Apologies! Sorry for shouting. My elevated excitement levels appear to be affecting some of my other functions.'

'That's OK. What's your name? And why are your excitement levels so high?' Marvin leant forward and patted the robot's smooth head.

'I am Pixel, a robot superhero sidekick. And you're my new superhero, my first superhero in years in fact. I can be a sidekick again. That is the current cause of my elevated excitement levels.'

Marvin laughed and shook his head.

'I'm Marvin. It's nice to meet you, but I'm no superhero.'

'That is incorrect data,' Pixel replied.

'No, you must be mistaken.' Marvin shook his head.

'My superhero detecting hardware might be, as you humans would say, rusty, but my readings are still showing a 99.99% chance that you're a superhero. There's very little chance that I'm wrong.'

'This is a mistake,' Marv said to himself, staring down at his shoes. 'I'll prove it to you. Come downstairs with me, and my grandad will tell you. I'm just an ordinary kid.'

Grandad clapped his hands in
delight the moment Marvin entered
with Pixel under his arm. He didn't seem
surprised at all to see Marvin wearing

the super-suit. Grandad pulled his
wallet out of his pocket and took an old
newspaper clipping out, handing it to
Marvin.

HERO SAVES TOWN AGAINST ODDS!

That was the headline. Beneath it, Marvin could see a real-life photo of Marv making a cool superhero pose. That face definitely looked familiar.

'Is that you?' Marvin said.

Grandad took off his sunglasses and put them on the table. His eyes were twinkling with delight. 'Yes, when I was all young and handsome. I was a superhero once upon a time. I packed my suit and sidekick away when I became too old and creaky to be a superhero. Your dad decided to become a different sort of hero, but I had always wondered whether you might wear the suit one day. You're named after me, after all! I had an inkling that one day you might carry on the name.'

Marvin just stood there. He didn't know what to say.

Pixel popped out of Marvin's arms and zipped over to Grandad. She beeped and rubbed herself against Grandad's leg. He patted her head. 'I'm so glad to see you again, Pixel. It's been too long,' Grandad said with a wide smile, then he turned back to Marvin. 'The suit is intelligent. It doesn't just work for anyone. If Pixel and that suit turned on for you, then it's for a reason.'

'But why?' Marvin said, even though deep down, he already knew the answer.

'Because you're a superhero, Marvin. Or should I say, Marv?' Grandad said with a grin.

CHAPTER 3

Marvin didn't know what to say. He had a million questions racing through his head all at once. He just didn't know where to start.

'So, what superpowers do you have, Grandad?' Marvin finally blurted out.

Grandad laughed.

'I don't have any, but that suit is something special.' Grandad pointed at Marvin's chest. 'It can do a great many things, and the more you wear it, the more you'll discover.'

Marvin looked down at the suit.

'But I don't have what it takes to be a real superhero,' he said.

'The suit is powered by two things: kindness and imagination. Luckily, you, little one, have tons of both!'

'But is it really that simple?' Marvin scratched at his head.

Grandad stood up, tutting.

'You just need to give the suit a go,

then you'll understand. Come with me.'
Grandad led Marvin to the back door. He
stepped outside while Marvin waited
nervously inside. 'Don't worry, it's dark
now—no one will see you,' Grandad called
out behind him. Marvin slowly stepped
out.

Grandad was right. The sky was dark
and filled with stars, the moon shining
brightly.

'Marvin—the sky's the limit if you
just believe in yourself,' Grandad said.
'Tell the suit what you want to try and
see what happens.'

Marvin looked up to the roof of their
house. He touched the 'M' on the front of
his suit.

'Walk on the wall . . . please,' Marvin whispered.

The suit whirred, and then small suction cups sprouted from his hands and feet. Marv felt like a robotic octopus!

'Woah! Marvin exhaled.

Marvin cautiously approached the wall, slowly lifting up his right foot and then stepping onto the wall. He wobbled his right leg, but it didn't move. It was stuck there.

Marvin took a deep breath, then yanked his left foot up and plopped it beside the other one. And just like that, Marvin's world was now sideways.

He took one step forward, then another. It worked! He was walking on the wall!

The suction cups on his feet knew precisely when to stop sticking and start sticking again. The suit was following his every want, without him even having ask. It was so cool!

Marvin's small steps quickly became long, confident strides, and in no time at all, he was standing on top of the roof.

The view was amazing! Marvin could see all the way to his school.

Down below, Grandad whooped and cheered while Pixel, who had followed them out in the garden, whizzed round in circles with excitement. Marvin's cheeks felt warm. He had really done it, all by himself. Marvin put his hands on his hips and struck a cool superhero pose.

He felt as though he could do anything! Marvin felt a surge of power through the suit and somersaulted and backflipped across the roof. This was nothing like his PE classes. Every move he made was perfect. He was so agile and well balanced, despite leaping across slippery roof tiles.

Marvin felt as though he could get used to this. He couldn't help but imagine how amazing he must have looked from down below. He could wear the suit to the Science Fair tomorrow and wow everyone. Just wait till Joe met Pixel! Just then, the whirring of the suit slowed down, and it began to splutter.

In an instant, Marvin's
excellent balance was gone.

'Argh!'

Marvin cried as he slipped
and began to fall. His heart hammered in
his chest.

'Use the suit!' Grandad shouted.

Marvin shot his hands forward, hoping for something—anything!—to happen. Ropes flew out of the sleeves of his suit and wrapped themselves around his house's drainpipe.

He jolted to a stop in mid-air and let out a deep breath.

Marvin used the ropes to slowly lower himself down to safety. He was back on the ground.

'Grandad, I think the suit is broken. It stopped working when I was on the roof,' Marvin cried.

'It's not broken. It just takes time to master,' Grandad chuckled. 'The suit is intelligent. It knows when it needs to be used and when you're just showing off,' he said with a grin. 'You'll get the hang of it.'

Marvin felt the suit crackle again and thought he could feel the power within. Grandad looked at Marvin and rubbed his chin thoughtfully.

'The world must be ready for a superhero, Marvin. Do you know what that means?' Grandad asked.

'No.' Marvin shook his head.

'The world must have a new supervillain,' Grandad said in a grave voice.

CHAPTER 4

The next morning, Marvin was packing his bag for the school Science Fair. It was heavier than usual because both Pixel and Marvin's super-suit were stuffed inside. Grandad told him to take them along 'just in case'.

Marvin was full of nervous energy.
Would today be the day he would get to
try being a superhero for real?

Marvin and Joe walked through
the double doors into the hall. Several
schools had entered the competition and
lively chatter filled the room.

SCIENCE FAIR

Marvin felt the excitement bubbling up in his chest. A quick glance at Joe and the wide smile on his face confirmed that Marvin wasn't the only one feeling excited.

All of a sudden, a shrill beeping came from Marvin's backpack. He swivelled around and gave a quick 'shhh'.

'Apologies, my excitement settings are proving difficult to regulate.' Pixel popped the top of her head out of the backpack, looking around the hall.

'It's OK, I just need you to be quiet and stay out of sight for a bit,' Marvin replied.

'Understood. Engaging high-tech stealth protocols,' Pixel said. She placed her hands in front of her face and then sank back into the backpack.

'What was that noise?' Joe asked.

'Nothing,' Marvin lied quickly. He wanted to tell Joe everything, but Grandad had warned him that superheroes should keep their identities a secret. So, he just let that secret bubble away inside him. 'Let's go find our table,' Marvin finally said. Joe nodded excitedly.

They made their way through the crowd, checking tables until they found one with their names on it.

Joe took out the Readaloud 3000 and put it down on the table, alongside the paper that the robot would be reading.

'Do you think it'll work?' Joe said nervously.

'I hope so!' Marvin replied.

Joe looked proudly at the robot. 'It had some great inventors.'

'Yeah, a great pair,' said Marvin.

All of a sudden, the lights in the hall went out. Marvin yelped. 'What's going on?'

An evil cackle filled the air. The sound came from the front of the hall, where the stage was. Marvin could just about see a shadowy figure standing on the stage. What was going on? Suddenly, a loud voice coming from the figure on the stage filled the air.

52

'The time has come to meet the winner of the Science Fair. ME!' the voice boomed. 'Be prepared to witness the power of my winning invention

mwahahahahahaha!'

There was a loud creaking sound and then a crash. A huge robot was smashing its way through one of the hall walls. It was gigantic! Bigger than any robot Marvin had ever seen before. Just the sight of it sent shivers up his spine.

Beams of light from the robot-shaped hole in the wall gave it a spotlight. It was made of dark steel carved into thick rectangles and squares, all except for its hands,

which were made of two rounded prongs.

People in the crowd screamed and began running away from the robot, looking for somewhere to hide.

Marvin ran over to the light switches and flipped them back on. When he turned around, Marvin could finally see the figure on the stage properly. It was a girl with bunches. She was wearing a long white lab coat with a giant 'M' on the front. She had a control panel in her hands and was cackling with glee. 'The time has come to surrender the Science Fair to me, supervillain MASTERMIND!' She pressed a button on the controls and the robot began swinging its arms around, wildly.

Mastermind cackled as she made her robot stomp around the hall. It crashed into people's tables, knocking over their inventions.

Marvin watched, confused. Was this what Grandad meant when he said that the world must have a new supervillain?

'Supervillain detected! Supervillain detected!' Pixel popped her head out of Marvin's backpack, her hands still over her face.

'I don't think you have to hide any more, Pixel,' Marvin said.

'Supervillain detected! Supervillain detected!' Pixel continued, lowering her hands.

Mastermind had to be stopped. Marvin gulped. It was time to test his powers out for real this time. Mastermind's robot was going to destroy the Science Fair. Marvin had to do something about it!

CHAPTER 5

'**E**RM . . . STOP!' Marvin shouted across the hall at Mastermind.

'Or what?' Mastermind laughed without even turning to look at him.

'I-I'll have to stop you,' Marvin stuttered.

'YOU?! STOP ME?!' Mastermind glanced at Marvin, then threw her head back and cackled. 'Look at you! You're no match for my giant robot!'

Marvin's head dropped. She was right. He was so small, and that robot was so big.

'Marvin! Help!' Joe cried. He was standing in front of their table protecting their invention from the robot now stomping its way towards him. Marvin gasped. He had to do something and fast.

Marvin turned and ran. Joe watched his best friend run away. 'Marvin! Where are you going?'

Marvin didn't have time to explain, and even though he felt a little bit scared, he knew what he had to do.

Marvin opened his backpack as he ran. 'Pixel, we have to stop Mastermind. Will you help me?'

'Of course. I have been programmed to do whatever I can to help superheroes stop supervillains,' Pixel replied solemnly, then paused. 'And on top of that this supervillain seems particularly annoying.'

'You're right.' Marvin smiled. 'Let's take Mastermind down and save the Science Fair!'

Marvin dashed outside the hall to change and returned a few moments later with Pixel hovering by his side. He was no longer Marvin. He was Marv!

Joe was bravely
protecting the Readaloud
3000 with his body and the
giant robot was almost upon him.

'MOVE DUMMY!' Mastermind
shouted to Joe. She hopped up and down
in frustration, her bunches swinging
back and forth. But Joe was
frozen to the spot.
His knees knocked
together, but his face
was stern.

The robot swung a giant arm down
and swiped at Joe, lifting him up in one
giant robotic hand.

'ARGGHHHHHH!' Joe cried.

Marv watched as Mastermind's jaw dropped. It was almost as though she hadn't been expecting that to happen. Mastermind was hammering at her controller and gritting her teeth. It wasn't working any more. She couldn't control the robot!

The giant robot swung its arms around wildly as it crashed around the hall—Joe still firmly in its grip.

'HEEELLLPPPP MEEEEE!' Joe yelled.

Marv knew he needed to stop the robot, but how? He put his hand over the 'M' symbol on his suit and tried to quiet his mind long enough to think about how he could defeat the out-of-control robotic beast. Then, an idea popped into his head.

Marv raced towards the robot; Pixel was right on his tail.

'IT'S SUPER-SUIT TIME!' Marv yelled as he got close to his target. 'Suction cups please activate!' The suction cups sprouted from the hands and feet of his suit. His heart pumped faster and faster and faster. His legs moved quicker than they had ever moved before. Marv couldn't keep the grin off his face. This is what it felt to be superpowered. It was awesome.

Marv leapt onto the back leg of the robot and scurried up towards the head. The robot gave a robotic roar and shook back and forth, trying to throw off Marv, but his suction cups kept him firmly on the robot's back. The robot's free hand swiped round to its back, trying to swat

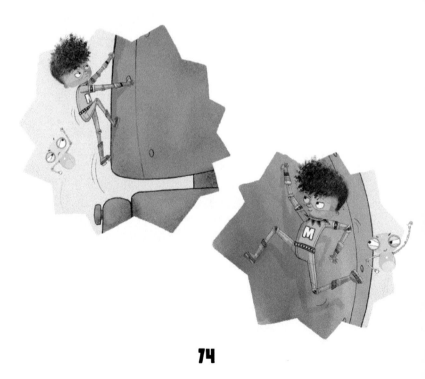

Marv off but he was too agile. Every time the robot's arm would take aim at Marv, he'd zip in the other direction just in the nick of time. And if it got too close, Pixel would reach out and zap it with electricity out of her hands.

'Who are you and what are you doing to MY robot!' Mastermind screeched.

'Erm . . . I am Marv. A superhero!'

Marv jumped around to the front of the robot and leapt onto the hand that held Joe in its grip. Before the robot could even react, Marv reached down and yanked at the robot's fingers with all his might. Marv could feel the super-strength surging into his arms and making his muscles more powerful than they had ever been before. The robotic

fingers creaked and then
popped out of place.
The robot roared again,
but there was nothing
it could do—Joe
was free of the robot's
grip and falling fast!
Marv grabbed Joe's hand
and swung him onto his back.
Joe should have been heavy,
but with Marv's super strength,
he felt light as a feather.
'Hold on,' Marv said. He tried
to make his voice sound
deeper than usual. Would
Joe guess it was him?

11

Marv turned
to the back of
the hall and
shot a long rope
from the arm of his suit. At
the end of the rope was a suction cup and
when it hit the ceiling, it fixed the rope in
place, letting Marv swing off the robot all
the way to the back of the hall.

'Woohoo!' Marv yelled as the wind whipped past his face.

Marv made a perfect landing and set
Joe down carefully on the ground.

'Thank you . . . thank you so much!' Joe
blurted out.

'You're welcome,' Marv nodded, still
trying to talk in a deep voice. 'Take care of
your invention, I hear it's a good one.'

'Don't worry, I will.' Joe replied, turning
to retrieve the Readaloud 3000, which had
somehow survived the carnage.

Joe ran off, and Marv turned back to the giant robot. It was stomping its way towards the Science Fair trophies! Steam was now hissing from the robot's back and neck, its arm swinging up and down in front of it. It looked as though it really wanted to smash up those trophies. Marv couldn't let that happen.

Marv's legs moved at super-speed as he headed back towards the robot. Marv reached for the robot's legs, shooting a piece of rope between them. He kept a hold of that rope as he sprinted in circles around the legs.

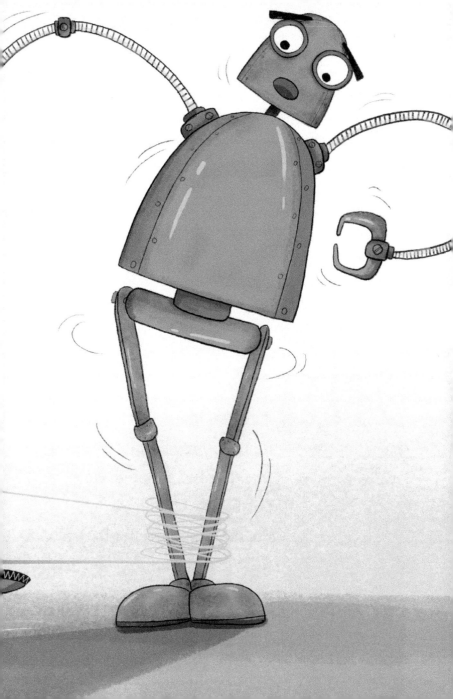

'Hey, Marv—get your hands off my robot!' Mastermind shouted. Now powerless, having thrown the robot's controller to the floor in frustration.

Marv ignored her. He pulled hard on the rope until it tightened. There was a high-pitch screeching as the robot's ankles were drawn together.

The huge robot wobbled one way, then the other.

Marv took a step
back. The robot's giant
shadow loomed over him.

'Based on my calculations I think
we should—' Pixel didn't get to finish.
Marv scooped her up in his arms and
then leapt out of the way.

The giant robot toppled over, smashing into the ground where they had been standing a moment before.

'As I was saying, based on my calculations I think we should move,' Pixel said.

'Yeah Pixel. I think you're right,' Marv replied with a smile.

CHAPTER 6

The giant robot was squirming on the floor, trying to get up. Marv and Pixel rushed over to it.

'Quick—let's try and put this robot out of action,' Marv said.

'Affirmative!' Pixel replied.

They searched the robot's giant body until they found a square steel cover.

'That appears to be the control panel,' Pixel said.

Marv gripped tight to the control panel's cover and pulled as hard as he could. It slowly bent, groaning as it crumpled up, then all at once it was ripped off. A mess of wires and plug holes were beneath it.

'Leave my robot alone!' Mastermind
yelled. Her face was bright red. It looked
as though at any moment, steam would
start coming out of her ears. Marv
ignored her.

'I don't really know how to turn it off.'
He turned to Pixel. 'Can you please help?'

Pixel opened a panel on her chest and pulled out a long wire with a plug at the end. 'I've heard humans say before, it takes a robot to beat a robot.'

'Humans say that?' Marv said, scratching his head.

'Of course they do,' Pixel said. She plugged herself into the control port and pressed a few buttons on the panel. A moment later, the robot stopped moving. It had been powered down.

'NOOOOOOOO!' shouted Mastermind.

Marv whipped around, ready to face Mastermind, but she was too fast for him.

A pair of rocket boosters sprung out of Mastermind's boots and flames erupted from them, powering her up and then towards the hole her robot had made in the wall.

'Suit! Quick! Activate rocket boosters,' Marv said, imagining catching Mastermind and the applause from the crowd as he brought her to justice. But nothing happened. 'Come on! Suit, activate rocket boosters!' Again, nothing happened. The suit began to make that weird spluttering sound, as it had done

the day before on his roof. The suit
wasn't going to work any more, and Marv
knew it.

'I'll catch you next time!' Marv
shouted.

Mastermind looked over her
shoulder and gave him a scowl.

'I hope your friend's invention comes
in millionth place!' she yelled.

'But that's impossible. There aren't

a million inventions here,' Marv said
scratching his head.

'Doesn't mattttteeeerrrr!'
Mastermind's voice echoed behind her
as she sped through the hole in the wall.

For a moment, all was still. The only
sound Marv could hear was his own
heavy breathing. Being a superhero was
tiring. Marv felt as though he wanted a
nap but that would have to wait.

People slowly came out of their hiding places, from underneath tables and chairs, and in no time at all, the hall was filled again. At first, they all just stared at Marv and Pixel. Then they began to clap. It started with just one person, but soon everyone in the room was clapping too. Some people even put their hands to their mouths and made high-pitched whistles.

Marv grinned so hard that his face hurt. His cheeks felt warm, and his chest felt fuzzy. He could have stood there for ever. Pixel tugged at the leg of Marv's suit. He looked down. There was a concerned look in her eyes. Marv nodded at her. She was right, it was time to leave.

Marv remembered what Grandad had said keeping his identity secret and leapt into action, running away from the crowd with Pixel by his side.

'That was amazing! Did you see how we saved everyone? It felt like we were real heroes.'

'I did say, I have a 99.99% correct superhero detector,' Pixel replied.

'That's true.' Marv smiled. 'Pixel, we are a superhero dream team! High five.'

'High five? That doesn't show up in any of my superhero databases. Is it a superpower?' Pixel said.

'Yes, the best power of all.

Friendship.' Marv reached back and
then lightly slapped Pixel's hand. 'High
five,' Marv said.

'I like that,' Pixel said, beeping
rapidly.

Once Marv had found a quiet spot
to change back into his normal clothes
and Pixel was safely inside
his bag, he made his way
back into the hall.

'And then he reached out and said, "take my hand". It was AWESOME!' Joe swung his arms wildly as he spoke, surrounded by his classmates who were listening to his every word. Marvin wriggled through the crowd and reached Joe.

Joe stopped talking the moment his eyes met Marvin's.

'Hey Joe, sorry for running away. I went to try and find help and I—' Marvin began to say, but Joe cut him off.

'Don't worry about it, Marvin,' Joe said with a shrug.

Marvin wasn't sure if Joe had truly forgiven him but he stepped back, and Joe got on with telling his story. In a couple of minutes, he was done, and the crowd left to clear up the mess the robot had made. Marvin and Joe went back to their table where their invention was sat unharmed.

Three judges walked from table to table, getting up close and looking over their glasses as they studied each

invention. Eventually they reached Marv
and Joe's table.

'And what do you have for us today?'
one of the judges said. His shirt was
untucked and his hair was messy.

Everyone had done their fair share of
running away from that giant robot,
but they were determined to judge the
competition all the same.

'Well—' Marvin cleared his throat.

'Wait, I have a new script,' Joe interrupted, switching the papers on the desk. Marvin raised his eyebrows. Joe hadn't told him about a new script.

'We'll let our invention speak for itself,' Joe said. Marvin reached forward and powered it on.

The tiny robot's head rose and the blue beams from its eyes scanned the paper. The judges leant forward. Marvin and Joe held their breath.

'Rule number 215 of the best friend code,' the robot said. The judges gasped, nodded, and frantically wrote things down on their clipboards. **'Best friends save each other when best friends are in danger.'** The robot finished then its head slumped down.

Marvin felt an elbow poke his side. He turned and Joe was looking at him with a funny expression. Was he joking or did he know that Marv was the one who had saved him? Joe winked and gave Marvin a smile.

The judges walked away from their table and on to the stage to announce the winners. Everyone left their tables and crowded around the stage. Marvin and Joe went with them. There was nervous chatter in the air.

'Do you think we've done enough to win it?' Joe whispered.

'I don't know, but I know we've done our best. That's what counts,' Marvin grinned.

'Yeah,' Joe replied.

The head judge stepped forward and tapped the mic.

'Hello, and thank you for attending this year's Science Fair. Of course, we had some . . . errrm . . . difficulties, but

thanks to the superhero known as Marv
we were able to resume the competition.
So, without further ado here are our
winners.' The crowd went quiet as the
judge spoke.

'In third place we have Sally
and Yinka with their nearly-empty-
toothpaste squeezer.' The crowd politely
clapped as two kids walked onto the
stage and received their prizes. Marvin's
stomach was performing backflips. So
they weren't in third place; maybe they
were higher, but maybe they were lower?

'In second place we have Benjamin and Ayo with their hot-soup blower. For people with sensitive mouths,' the judge said. The crowd politely clapped again. Joe gripped Marvin's shoulder.

So, they weren't second or third place, there was only one other opportunity to win a prize. 'And finally, the winner of this year's Science Fair is . . .' The judge paused. Marvin couldn't breathe. 'The Readaloud 3000!'

Marvin stood there for a second, eyes wide and mouth open. Did they really just say what he thought they just said? Joe dragged Marvin out of his thoughts and up onto the stage. Marvin stood there, with a smile that felt as though it would never leave his face. The crowd around them clapped hard and whistled.

It was the second time that day that Marvin had been in front of a cheering crowd. Last time he had been Marv the superhero and this time he was Marvin the boy. He turned and grinned at his best friend. Being a superhero was cool, but being an ordinary boy was pretty great too!

ABOUT THE AUTHOR

ALEX FALASE-KOYA

Alex is a London native. He has been both
reading and writing since he was a teenager
and was a winner of Spread the Word's 2019
London Writers Awards for YA and Children's.
He now lives in Walthamstow with his
girlfriend and two cats.

ABOUT THE ILLUSTRATOR

PAULA BOWLES

Paula grew up in Hertfordshire, and has always loved drawing, reading, and using her imagination, so she studied illustration at Falmouth College of Arts and became an illustrator. She now lives in Bristol, and has worked as an illustrator for over ten years, and has had books published with Nosy Crow and Simon & Schuster.

MARV

Marvin's life changed when he found an old superhero suit and became MARV. The suit has been passed down through Marvin's family and was last worn by his grandad. It's powered by the kindness and imagination of the wearer and doesn't work for just anybody.

COURAGE	7
FRIENDSHIP	9
KINDNESS	9
POWERS	10
AGILITY	7
COMBAT SKILLS	6

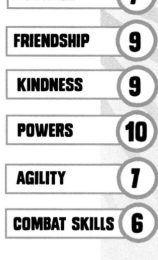

PIXEL

PIXEL is Marv's brave superhero sidekick. Her quick thinking and unwavering loyalty make her the perfect crime-fighting companion.

COURAGE	6
FRIENDSHIP	10
KINDNESS	9
POWERS	5
AGILITY	7
COMBAT SKILLS	5

MASTERMIND

MASTERMIND is a genius who can create amazing inventions. She doesn't have any superpowers, but is incredible at science and engineering. She'd love to take over the world with an army of evil robots.

COURAGE	5
FRIENDSHIP	4
KINDNESS	4
POWERS	6
AGILITY	6
COMBAT SKILLS	6

'THE SUPER-SUIT IS POWERED BY TWO THINGS:
KINDNESS AND **IMAGINATION.**
LUCKILY YOU, MARVIN, HAVE TONS OF BOTH!'

LOVE MARV?
WHY NOT TRY THESE TOO...?